Christmas Moon

Christmas Moon

Denys Cazet

BRADBURY PRESS   NEW YORK

Bradbury Press
An Affiliate of Macmillan, Inc.
866 Third Avenue, New York, N.Y. 10022
Collier Macmillan Canada, Inc.

Manufactured in the United States of America.
10 9 8 7 6 5 4 3 2
The text of this book is set in 16 pt. Goudy Old Style. The illustrations are drawn in ink with watercolor wash, reproduced in full color.
Library of Congress Cataloging in Publication Data
Cazet, Denys.
   Christmas moon.
   Summary: Patrick misses Grandpa, especially at Christmas, but his mother helps him to remember happy times with Grandpa and to use what Grandpa taught him to make Christmas happy for himself and his friends.
   1. Children's stories, American. [1. Death—Fiction.
2. Grandfathers—Fiction. 3. Christmas—Fiction]
I. Title
PZ7.C2985Ch   1984   [E]   84-10969
ISBN 0-02-717810-2

for the man in the moon, G.M.L.

Patrick couldn't sleep.

The moon filled the room with long shadows. The curtains stirred and Grandpa's old rocking chair creaked slowly back and forth.

Patrick turned on the light.

He rubbed his eyes and stared at Grandpa's picture for a
long time.

"Patrick," whispered Mother. "What's the matter?"
"My head is full of Grandpa," Patrick said sadly.

Mother sat on the edge of the bed. "It's Christmas Eve," she said, fluffing up the pillow. "Let's try not to be sad."

"Before Grampa died, I wasn't sad," said Patrick.

"I miss him, too," said Mother.

Patrick nodded. "Do you think Grandpa is sad, like me?"

"When Grandpa felt sad," Mother said, "he used moon magic to chase the sadness away."

"He did?"

"That's what he told me."

"Secret magic?" asked Patrick.

"Very secret."

"So secret you can't tell me?" Patrick whispered.

"So secret I must tell you!"

Patrick looked out the window. "Can you use the
Christmas moon?"

"The Christmas moon is the most magical of all."

"Does it work?" Patrick asked.

"Well, let's see." Mother turned off the light.

She waved her hand through the moonlight and wiggled her fingers over Patrick.

She ran her fingers through his hair and hugged him tightly.
She kissed him on the cheek.

"Moon magic," said Mother.

"Did Grandpa show you?" asked Patrick.

"Yes, when I was little," Mother said, "just like he showed you how to ride your bicycle."

"Grandpa said I was the best bicycle rider he ever saw."
"I remember."

"Remember when Grandpa took me to the carnival? He bet
me he could hit the bell with the big hammer and I couldn't."

"I won," Patrick said proudly. "But you know what? I think
Grandpa lost on purpose."

"Sounds like Grandpa."

"When I was with Grandpa," said Patrick, "I didn't feel little."

"And how do you feel now?"

"Not so little!"

"Good," Mother said. "Because tomorrow is a big day.
While I'm cooking, I'll need you to help me with the little kids."

"I know," said Patrick. "I'll show Louie's little sister how to
ride my bicycle."

"I think she'll like that!"
"I can run races and let the littlest one win!" Patrick said.
Mother smiled and tucked Patrick under the covers.
"Goodnight, Patrick."
"Goodnight, Mother."

Patrick closed his eyes.
"Merry Christmas," he whispered.

Patrick closed his eyes.
"Merry Christmas," he whispered.